BILLY LTI
and his
Magical Trip

*For Blake
Happy Reading
Best
Richard Guimond
2014*

Written by Richard Guimond
and Woody Woodman

Original story by Woody Woodman

Illustrated by Woody Woodman

Library of Congress Control Number: 2013910313
CreateSpace Independent Publishing Platform, North Charleston, South Carolina

Contents

Lighthouse

O n this very bright and salty day, Billy Pip, a freckled nine-year-old boy with light blond hair, watched curiously as an unexpected fog bank approached the rocky Maine shoreline. Billy who always wore rubber boots, a rain jacket, and a yellow hat—whether it was raining or not, was an avid reader. Wherever he went, he carried a book bag filled with his favorite adventure stories.

Billy opened his bag and took out *Treasure Island*. He loved *Treasure Island* more than any other story. His mind wandered as he flipped through the pages of his favorite pirate tale.

Surrounded by the big, blue Atlantic Ocean, Billy was very proud of his well-kept dinghy. He smiled at his miniature toy cannon fastened to the stern of his little boat. He found comfort there, especially today, in the warm sun and constant briny breeze.

Off in the distance, he heard the faint sound of a ship's bell.

He cried out, "Pirate ship off starboard side. Make ready the cannons!"

"Aye, aye, Captain! We'll soon be alongside those scallywags!"

He jumped up and brandished his wooden sword. The boat rolled slightly, and he could hear the cries of hungry seagulls and the loud roar of ocean waves as they crashed against the shore. He barked out the orders: "Captain! Those scallywags are making a run for it! Let's go after them!"

Billy quickly sat down and pretended to row his boat.

"Prepare to fire! Aye, aye, Captain!" Billy responded excitedly.

Another ship's bell clanged, but this one was louder and closer. He turned toward the shore and the cottage where he and his mother lived. The cottage was nestled alongside a very tall lighthouse.

The sound of that ship's bell snapped him back to reality. Billy was nowhere near the ocean; his small row-boat padlocked to a large anchor in the back-yard rested on a log and gently rolled with Billy's every move.

Scattered about in the skiff were his favorite adventure novels, an atlas, and an animal reference book.

Billy's mother, Margaret, nicknamed Maggie, had just rung the ship's bell outside the cottage door. For a long time now, they had lived a quiet, rather isolated existence as lighthouse keepers. Maggie had the enormous responsibility of looking after the signal beacon for the Coast Guard.

Heading toward Billy with a tray of milk and cookies, his mom was a pretty woman with long reddish-brown hair. Today she was wearing a dress covered in bright yellow-and-white daisies.

Billy stood up and shouted, "Ahoy, Mom! Look at me—I am fighting off the pirates! Wait! I'll fire the cannon and scare them off for good." He leaned over and pushed the plunger on his toy cannon. There was a small puff of smoke and a pathetic little *pop*.

Billy's mother smiled as she approached the boat.

She set the tray down on the seat and saluted her son. "Permission to come aboard, Captain?"

Billy returned the salute. "Permission granted, Mom."

His mother smiled again. Yes, they had played this game before.

She climbed into the boat and sat alongside her son. He tried to grab a cookie, but she gently pushed his hand away.

She took a bar of soap and a washcloth from her apron. "A clean ship is a happy ship, Billy."

"Yes, Mother, I remember." Billy took the soap and stuck his hands in a bucket of water.

Looking out over the ocean, she said, "The fog is coming in earlier than I expected today. I'll need to turn on the beacon soon."

"Yeah, Mom, it is our job to keep the fishermen and boaters safe."

With much love in her pale blue eyes, she reminded Billy in a gentle but firm voice, "You always must respect the power of the ocean."

Billy dried his hands and replied, "I know, Mother, and the ocean can be *sooo* dangerous." However, his tone of voice made it clear that he did not agree. "But it's still exciting to dream about a great ocean adventure, don't you think?"

His mother's expression softened as she handed him a cookie and a glass of milk.

She turned back toward the ocean. "Remember, Billy, dreaming can lead to doing. Promise me you will never go out on the ocean alone. You know what happened to your father."

Billy gave his mother a nod, and she could see that he was thinking about her remark. He picked up the novel on the seat beside him and said, "I like the boy in *Treasure Island*, Mom. Jim Hawkins isn't afraid of the ocean. He's young, like me, and loves lots of adventures."

He saw that she was genuinely concerned. He

forced a small smile and saluted her. "Don't worry; I would probably get seasick anyway."

Lifting up his hat, she gave him a kiss. As she walked back to their cottage, she turned and waved to her son.

Billy stretched out in his dinghy and stared up at the fluffy white clouds. He imagined all the different characters and faraway lands from the stories he had read—some funny some scary. He wondered if he would ever get to visit those places. Before he closed his eyes, he said aloud, "I wish I could have a real adventure."

The sun slowly disappeared behind the rolling blanket of fog that surrounded Billy and his boat.

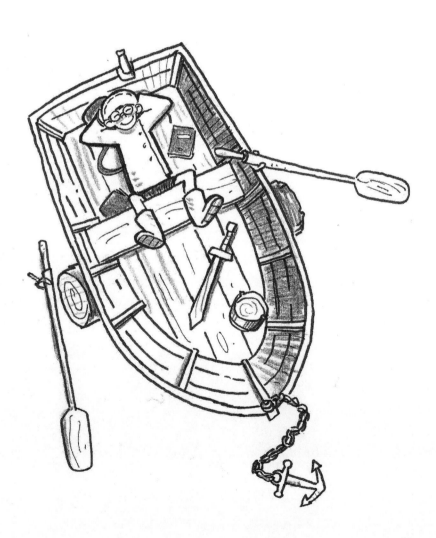

Meet the Crew

While Billy slept, he could hear the wail of a foghorn and what sounded like voices in the distance.

Billy realized they were the salty words of the pirates from *Treasure Island*. "Shiver me timbers. Fifteen men on the dead man's chest. Yo-ho-ho…"

A moment later, he heard the irritating squawks of a parrot. "Pieces of eight! Pieces of eight!"

A spray of cold seawater splashing over his face jolted Billy awake. He found himself in the middle of the ocean; and his boat was dangerously taking on water.

He knew immediately the heavy anchor that was still chained to its bow was pulling it down. He tried to bail out the boat, but he couldn't keep up with the water. It was a very desperate situation.

He stuck his hands into the ocean and tried to remember the numbers to the combination lock. "Right, seven; left two times, four; back right to eight. No! No! It's left two times, five; back right to eight. No! No!"

Things were quickly going from bad to worse. Billy could not believe what was happening: hungry sharks surrounded his boat. One fin followed by another and yet another circled the boat.

In all this chaos, he slipped and whacked his arm on the cannon, and it fired—*pop!*

Just as the sharks were getting more aggressive, Billy looked around for his sword and saw it drifting away.

Using one of his oars, he slapped at the water, trying to scare the sharks, but they didn't pay much attention to him.

Billy turned, and through the fog he could see the beacon from the lighthouse. As seawater continued to flood the boat, he frantically paddled toward the shore.

Suddenly, the oar snapped in two. He lifted up the remaining half, stared, and mumbled to himself, "I think I'm gonna need a bigger boat!"

Overhead, Billy heard a loud boom. He looked up and realized a fishing net had scooped him up. As he felt himself being lifted into the air, the dinghy slowly sank beneath him. *Glup, glup, glup.* He felt for his book bag and was relieved to find it snug across his shoulder.

As he was being hoisted up, Billy caught the name of the rescue boat: USS *Hope*. The net swung in a circle and left him suspended upside down over the deck.

Billy couldn't believe what stood before him. Through the net, he eyed one very large and oddly dressed man. This had to be the Captain. He was wearing a white skipper's cap, a jacket covered in ribbons and medals, a green-and-blue Scottish

kilt, and cowboy boots. He sported a big red moustache that went from ear to ear. And even though it was daylight, he was carrying a lantern.

Perched on the Captain's shoulder was a one-eyed crow, squawking and flapping his wings. "Don't mind One-Eyed Jack. His squawk is worse than his bite," shouted the Captain.

The crow's only eye seemed to sparkle at the Captain's comment.

With a huge pipe clenched between his teeth, the Captain leaned down into Billy's face. "Well, you ain't exactly the catch of the day."

Billy was too frightened and confused to say anything. He was having a hard time adjusting to this situation.

"Look, boy, I'm master and commander of the USS *Hope*. She is the finest fishing vessel in all the seven seas. They call me Captain Big Red Curtis"—he paused for a moment—"although I'm not sure why they call me that."

Billy stuttered and said, "Bi-Bil-Billy, sir. Billy Pip."

The Captain grunted. "Who? What did you say?"

The Captain's lantern brightened momentarily.

"That's my name, sir. Billy Pip. Permission to come aboard?" Still hanging upside down in the net, Billy managed to salute the Captain.

"Permission granted." The Captain released the net, dropping Billy and his book bag onto the deck, alongside a heap of flapping fish. Billy jumped away and slipped backward onto the wet deck.

For a moment, he just sat there among the flipping, twisting fish.

The Captain shook his head. "Come with me."

Billy was confused. "Sir?"

Captain Curtis had no problem moving about on the pitching deck. He walked and rolled with the ocean as though he had suction cups on his boots. Even the crow swayed back and forth with the Captain.

As Billy tried to follow, the Captain continued to blabber away. He wasn't paying any attention to Billy, nor was the boy paying any attention to the Captain.

Billy did his best to follow the Captain. He grabbed and held tight to the rigging as the boat rocked and rolled.

"Well, Billy Pip, I'm on a mission, and this interference has cost me some time. You have ruined my chances of catching Sissy today."

"Sir, you see, I was safely sleeping in my row-boat, when somehow I got swept out to sea. You see, I promised my mother…"

The Captain ignored Billy as he continued his tour of the boat. "Stern is back there, and the bow is the front. Port is left, and starboard is the right side. Mid-ship is where we're standing. Below-decks are the galley and the fish hold. It's all pretty standard stuff."

"I was never allowed to go near the ocean, and my mother would never allow me out on an actual fishing boat."

The Captain pointed to a hatch and a ladder leading to the lower deck. "Down there is the fish hold. That will be your sleeping quarters. That is the only area of the boat that you are allowed to occupy."

"Occupy?" Confused, Billy slipped on the wet deck and palmed the slimy wall of the pilothouse. He was completely grossed out by the fish slime that was now on his hand. He wiped it on his sleeve as he watched the crow fly into the pilothouse.

The Captain leaned down into Billy's face. "And what your hand just touched happens to be my pilothouse, which is completely off limits to you! Understand?"

Billy nodded, but he was suddenly spooked as One-Eyed Jack squawked at him, "Off limits! Off limits!"

Billy fell back and nearly went overboard, but the Captain caught him and laughed. "One-Eyed Jack will grow on you."

"Yes, sir! I hope so, sir!"

"Now, Billy, best you be working on those sea legs if you're gonna be around long enough to catch what we're fishing for."

"Like I was saying, sir, I was under attack from a school of sharks."

The Captain shook his head. "For Pete's sake, boy! Haven't you heard a word I've said? Those fins weren't sharks! They were the backside of Sissy the Sea Serpent's tail. We are hunting a dragon, boy!"

Billy's expression turned fearful. "A dragon? I need to go home."

"Impossible!" the Captain said loudly.

They walked up to the bow. Bolted down in front of the pilothouse was a cannon. Billy pointed to what looked like a harpoon inside the large barrel. "What's that?"

"Harpoon, net, and cannon."

"What do you use that for?"

"Odds and ends," replied the Captain.

Squawking like a parrot, One-Eyed Jack flew back onto the Captain's shoulder.

Billy thought about the parrot in his dream: *Pieces of eight! Pieces of eight!*

One-Eyed Jack screeched, "Set him adrift! Set him adrift! Catching a dragon!" He squawked once more, "Catching a dragon…"

One-Eyed Jack pecked at Billy's glasses as though he wanted to steal them. While he flapped his wings, Billy glimpsed a small, stuffed leather pouch beneath his right wing.

The Captain pointed up to the mast and then to the crow's one eye. "Get up in the crow's nest, Jack, and keep your only sharp eye open."

Shaking his head and shooing the bird away, Billy watched One-Eyed Jack fly up the mast. "What kind of boat is this, anyway?"

The Captain rubbed his chin and said, "Well, Billy, the USS *Hope* isn't like other ships."

Billy mumbled, "You can say that again."

Up in the mast, One-Eyed Jack squawked like a parrot, "You can say that again!"

"Here's what I mean, Billy: the USS *Hope* is a special ship. She can do anything and take you anywhere you want to go."

"I really want to go home."

The Captain stood over Billy. "No! Your mother wants you home…because the world is *sooo* dangerous."

Billy was very puzzled. "But how do you know?"

The Captain grabbed Billy and pulled him up. "Trust me, boy, all mothers are like that."

On the starboard side, something jumped out of the water and made a loud clicking sound.

"Oh, we're in luck! See that mermaid?"

"You mean that dolphin?"

The Captain mumbled in frustration and cleared his throat. "Her name is Love!" The Captain went down on one knee and rolled up his sleeve, revealing a mermaid tattoo. "We'll follow her."

Then he rolled up his other sleeve and showed Billy a fairy tattoo. "You see, Faith is a fairy…" He lifted up the lantern. "Billy, in this lantern is Faith, and as long as we travel with Hope and follow Love, Faith will light the way and no harm can come to us."

Billy mumbled, "I don't understand, sir."

The Captain shook his head. "Don't worry, you'll figure it out as we go along." He extended his hand. "Whaddaya say, kid? You gonna be my first mate?"

Billy thought about it for a moment. "If I help you catch the dragon, will you take me home?"

"Safe and sound, before your mother even knows you're missing."

The Captain snuffed up a big batch of spit from his throat and coughed into his hand. "Put 'er there, First Mate." He offered his big, clammy hand to Billy.

Billy, disgusted by the sight of the Captain's dripping fingers, slowly extended his own hand.

"Ahhh, first you have to spit on it. Really dig deep from the back of your throat." Billy tried to draw up from his lungs but managed only to dribble out a bit of spit.

The Captain shouted enthusiastically, "Good enough!" They shook hands. "We start at first light."

Billy grimaced and wiped the goop off his hand. He glanced around the boat and felt very small in this enormous ocean. Looking up at the Captain, he asked, "Sir, about how long will this dragon hunting take?"

"Twenty-five years."

Billy turned around and threw up overboard.

From the crow's nest, Billy heard One-Eyed Jack squawking, "Set him adrift! Set him adrift! Catching a dragon…"

Shipshape

Down in the fish hold, gently rolling with the boat, Billy slept soundly in his hammock. He was tired, and despite the clammy cold of the fish hold, he liked the warmth and snugness of the hammock. Perched on a nearby bench was an old deep-sea-diving suit. It appeared to be waiting for orders.

From up on deck, One-Eyed Jack broke the quiet with his version of a bugle call.

Billy's eyes jerked open as a bucket of cold seawater drenched him. As if in a bad dream, he fell out of the hammock. But it was the Captain's voice that truly startled him. "First light, First Mate! First light!"

Spitting water, Billy jumped to attention. He stood there soaking wet. He quickly put on his glasses and noticed that the dive suit was now on the other side of the bench.

From topside, One-Eyed Jack continued squawking, "First light! Squawk! First light!"

The Captain stood over Billy with a mop and a bucket. "Remember, a clean ship is a happy ship."

"Hey, my mom says that!"

Handing him the mop, Captain Curtis nodded. "After all, this is where you'll be sleeping."

In the fish hold, Billy scrubbed the floor and the walls and anything else that needed cleaning. While he worked, he felt as if someone were watching him. He

kept glancing over his shoulder at the dive suit. Yes indeed, there was something strange about that dive suit.

When he turned around, the suit had moved back to the other side of the bench. Billy's eyes widened in apprehension. As the ship rolled again, he watched the suit slide back to its original position. Relieved, he went back to work scrubbing the fish hold.

When he had finished his chores and was ready to jump into his hammock for a nap, he found that the dive suit was already there. Screaming, he climbed out of the fish hold and onto the main deck.

He shouted to the Captain, "What's up with the creepy dive suit?"

In the pilothouse, a smiling Captain Curtis shouted back, "Don't worry, First Mate! Davey's part of the crew! And now, since you're up here, swab the deck!"

Billy, despite the fact that One-Eyed Jack was pestering him, didn't mind the work. When he was tossing the last bucket of soapy water overboard, he missed and soaked the crow instead. Captain Curtis laughed, and One-Eyed Jack squawked wildly.

At lunchtime, Billy sat down on the forward deck to a big bowl of fish and rice. While he ate, he watched Love swimming ahead of the USS *Hope*; apparently, the bottle-nosed dolphin was guiding the ship on its journey. Every now and then, Billy flipped through his animal book, looking at pictures of dolphins. He learned that they were quite intelligent and very friendly.

By late afternoon, Billy was hanging from the rigging and painting the mast. With the paint bucket harnessed to his waist, he was enjoying his new position as first mate.

Climbing down from the mast, Billy was covered in white paint. From out of nowhere, One-Eyed Jack swooped down and snatched Billy's glasses. The bird quickly flew back up into his nest.

Billy looked up. "Come back here, you little thief!"

He climbed back up the ladder to the crow's nest, and, much to his surprise, he discovered One-Eyed Jack's nest of shiny trinkets. Billy glared at the crow. "So *that's* what you hide in your little leather pouch."

One-Eyed Jack blinked his good eye and squawked. Billy reached into the stash for his eyeglasses, and the two immediately began to struggle. As they tussled, the bird squawked loudly. The more they wrestled, the more they became entangled in the boat's rigging.

In a matter of minutes, Billy was hanging upside down, and the paint bucket that had been tied to his waist had dropped to the deck. A second later, One-Eyed Jack popped out of the bucket, covered in white paint.

From the pilothouse, Captain Curtis pointed his finger at Billy. "Quit playing around. Get cleaned up, and meet me in the engine room!"

Later, Billy climbed down into the engine room. Holding the lantern, the Captain opened the door.

Billy was overwhelmed by the noise, the smell, and the soot in the engine room. The Captain handed Billy some earmuffs that would protect his ears from the noise.

The Captain pointed to the coal-fired steam engine.

Surprised to see a roaring fire inside the ship's boiler, Billy looked around the engine room and noticed that the walls were covered with soot. He already knew what his next job would be.

The Captain hung the lantern on a nearby hook and ran his finger along the wall, removing a thick layer of dirt.

Billy just nodded and went to work.

When the job was done, Billy emerged from the engine room, and from head to toe he was as black as One-Eyed Jack.

On the deck, the crow lay on his back, cracking up. Every time he stopped laughing, he pointed his wing at Billy and started laughing all over again.

The Captain, grabbed Faith in one hand, and used his free hand to remove Billy's soot-covered glasses.

Briefly, Billy saw a faint image dancing in the lantern. Puzzled, he reached for his glasses and saw that it was only a flame. He shrugged to himself.

Captain Curtis, with the crow back on his shoulder and carrying the lantern, returned to the pilothouse.

Billy scratched his head. "What a strange boat." He finally finished his work and went topside. Standing in the doorway of the pilothouse, Billy asked, "Permission to wash up and go to bed? I need to rest."

The Captain responded, "Permission granted. Tomorrow is another big day!"

Love Returns

The next day, the USS *Hope* was anchored in a calm sea. Captain Curtis stared down as a stream of air bubbles plopped to the ocean's surface. On the side of the boat was a safety line with an air hose running, and Billy Pip was surprised to find himself wearing Davey's dive suit and scraping barnacles from the ship's bottom.

Billy was wondering what his mother would have thought about his newfound bravery. Wearing not only his glasses but Davey's helmet, too, Billy noticed that the little fish around him appeared gigantic.

He watched a jellyfish drift by and attach itself to the helmet. He thought the jellyfish's pulsing body resembled a slow-motion dance. Billy gently touched the jellyfish, and it quickly swam away, waving its tentacles in a good-bye salute.

Billy smiled and returned the wave. Despite being underwater, he felt at ease.

On the deck, Captain Curtis continued to keep a watchful eye. However, One-Eyed Jack, always mischievous, was playing with the valve to Billy's air supply.

Captain Curtis immediately shooed the bird away.

Hard at work, Billy was distracted by a small octopus that had latched onto his arm. Billy tickled the creature, and it swam away, leaving a jet of ink in its wake.

As Billy's eyes followed the octopus, the reflection of a pretty girl's face appeared out of nowhere in the glass of the diver's helmet. Startled by the sight, he quickly turned around and got a glimpse of a large, gleaming tail fin swimming away.

Suddenly, Billy felt like he was running out of air, and the helmet began to fog up. He headed for the surface but slammed into the bottom of the boat. He saw stars for a moment but quickly popped up alongside the ship.

Captain Curtis helped him climb up the ladder and remove the helmet. Billy was as red as a strawberry, and his glasses were all fogged up.

The Captain glanced at a guilty-looking Jack, who was standing on the air valve again. Captain Curtis removed Billy's glasses and said, "Well done, for your first dive…Next time we'll keep One-Eyed Jack tied up in the fish hold!"

Billy took a deep, frustrated breath and glanced over the side. He saw that the USS *Hope* glistened like a diamond on the sea. Still catching his breath, he said, "I think I saw a mermaid."

"Oh, that was Love," the Captain replied, as a dolphin, clicking and squealing with delight, jumped high into the air.

Billy, looking puzzled, removed Davey the dive suit and left it on the deck to dry.

He followed the mumbling captain up to the pilothouse but stopped short of the door.

Billy looked back at the dive suit, and except for wet footprints leading back to the fish hold, it was gone.

The Captain glanced down at an ocean chart and tapped his finger a few times.

"Take the wheel, Billy! I need to speak with Love."

"But you told me never to go into the pilothouse."

The Captain replied, "Don't listen to everything I say!"

Billy grabbed the steering wheel.

Captain Curtis bolted from the pilothouse and ran up onto the bow as if his kilt were on fire. He whistled, and the dolphin immediately chattered back. "What do you mean, the trail has run dry? It's the Atlantic Ocean, for crab's sake! It's all wet!"

The dolphin squealed and dove beneath the waves.

From the crow's nest, One-Eyed Jack squawked, "Run dry! Run dry!"

The Captain returned to the pilothouse steaming mad. For a moment, he stared at Billy's hands locked on the steering wheel. "I thought I told you never to touch that, boy! Only the Captain can steer this boat!"

Billy looked flabbergasted at the Captain. "But, sir, you just told me to—"

"Stow it, First Mate! I'm trying to think."

Billy muttered to himself while Captain Curtis rubbed his chin, deep in thought.

Above in the crow's nest, One-Eyed Jack blabbered away. He flew into the pilothouse, landed on the Captain's shoulder, and squawked, "Land ho! Land ho!"

Billy's eyes lit up.

"Thank you, Jack, but I'm capable of addressing the crew myself. Back to your post!"

One-Eyed Jack tilted his head at Billy, who quickly removed his glasses so the bird couldn't steal them again.

Captain Curtis turned to Billy. "We're going ashore."

Going Ashore

After docking the boat inside a small harbor, Billy couldn't wait to feel solid ground beneath him. He grabbed his book bag, looked at the Captain, and asked, "Permission to go ashore, sir?"

"Permission granted, First Mate."

Billy jumped onto the wharf, and it felt so good that he knelt down and kissed the ground. As they walked around the busy pier, Billy heard the fishermen calling out to the Captain. He realized that the Captain was quite well-known. Mending nets, one of the fishermen called out, "Hey! Big Red, where have you been?"

Another fisherman yelled, "Big Red is still chasing the tail of that dragon."

Captain Curtis replied, "Your boat still leaks, and you're still chasing mackerel."

From the USS *Hope*'s mast, One-Eyed Jack mimicked the fisherman. "Chasing his dragon! Squawk! Chasing his dragon!"

Captain Curtis shrugged. "Sometimes that bird gets on my nerves."

The Captain pointed to a woman filleting fish. "That's Sally Three Fingers. Sally doesn't see too well and keeps cutting herself. If you want to keep all your fingers, keep your hands in your pockets."

Billy immediately tucked his hands into his rain slicker.

"That reminds me, Billy Pip. Seeing that you're my first mate, I have a little present for you."

"A present?"

The Captain removed a pocketknife from his jacket. "Sometimes you'll have a need for a knife, especially to cut rope or mend nets. All first mates need a knife."

For a moment, Billy stared at the jackknife, deep in thought. He dug into his pocket and pulled out a coin. He handed a penny to the Captain, who smiled and responded, "Well, I see you know the secret to a seaman's trade. How'd you learn that?"

"From one of my books, sir!"

Captain Curtis nodded approvingly.

A group of kids ran up to the Captain and circled him like bees after honey.

"Hey, Captain Curtis, did you catch the dragon?"

The Captain replied, "No, but I caught myself a first mate!"

"That doesn't count. We want the dragon!"

In response, the Captain ripped a loud one. "*Brrrrrrrrrrrrrrrrr!*" Laughing, the kids all ran away, holding their noses.

Captain Curtis glanced at Billy, who was also laughing, and said, "Rule number one for hunting dragons, son: be friendly, but avoid the tail winds."

Billy and the Captain shared a big belly laugh.

They walked side by side through the busy market.

The Captain appeared to know the area well. Billy held his nose and poked at the fish in the carts. "Smells fishy to me!"

"Well, First Mate, we ain't here to buy fish that we can catch at sea."

"Then why are we here?"

Captain Curtis pointed to a white-bearded fisherman slumped over a fish barrel. As they approached the man, the Captain grabbed a flounder from a nearby basket and slapped the man silly with the wet fish. "Wake up, Foggy Joe!"

The man opened his eyes. "Why, Captain Curtis, I was just dreaming about catching a boatload of mackerel, and you spoiled my catch."

Captain and Foggy Joe shook hands, and the old fisherman looked at Billy and offered his dirty hand.

Billy reluctantly shook his hand and then quickly rinsed his in a nearby bucket of water.

Captain Curtis asked, "Foggy Joe, have you seen anything unusual lately?"

The old fisherman's eyes ignited. Even his white beard stood on end. He took off his cap and wiped his brow in one motion. He jumped up like a jack-in-the-box, and his words came out faster than a locomotive. "As a matter of fact, last night I saw a monstrous fish. It had a long body like an eel, covered with scales and fins. It was enormous! It was one very scary sight!"

The Captain glanced at Billy and nodded.

Billy looked questionably at Foggy Joe. He clearly didn't believe what the old man was saying.

Billy reached into his bag and opened one of his animal books; he found nothing that resembled what Foggy Joe had just described. He shrugged and closed the book.

In the harbor, unknown to them, a large sea creature gently broke the water's surface and swam around the USS *Hope*.

"Well, Billy, Foggy Joe has more knowledge than all those books put together." The Captain turned back to the old man. "Are you sure that's what you saw?"

The old man became annoyed. "Just a minute—I know what I saw, Captain Curtis. At times I may be swamped, stewed, and soaked, but I ain't ever lost my dinghy."

Billy whispered to the Captain, "A dinghy is a boat."

With that, Foggy Joe climbed into the fish barrel and fell back to sleep.

"Let's move on, Billy. Old Foggy needs to inspect his eyelids."

Billy said, "He is sure is a strange duck."

"More like a strange fish, Billy. You see, Foggy Joe has been through so much, sometimes he sees more than just sea serpents. He's been known to see pink elephants dancing over the ocean."

Billy shook his head.

The Captain said, "We need to get to the bottom of this."

Before they headed back to the ship, the Captain bought a lemon at the produce stand and handed it to Billy. "Slice off a piece with your new knife and suck on it—it will help you get your sea legs."

Billy stared at the lemon slice and made a face. He shook his head. "Sorry, sir, I just can't do it."

The Captain shrugged. "It's your belly."

Heading back to the ship, the Captain and Billy waved good-bye to Sally Three Fingers and all the children.

Sally yelled over to the Captain, "Hey, Big Red, Pedro the chicken man and his wife might know something about what you're searching for. They aren't too far from here."

"Thanks, Sally. I think I know where to find them."

A bit later, the USS *Hope* was making her way back, when the seas became a little rough. Billy got seasick, and the next thing he knew, he was hanging over the side of the boat.

Arriving at the next harbor over, the Captain tied up at the town dock. As soon as the boat stopped rocking, Billy began feeling better. He was more than happy to get back on solid ground. The pair got off the ship and continued their search for clues.

Approaching a small farmhouse, the Captain and Billy found a woman busy hanging her laundry. The Captain removed his hat, and Billy followed. "Pardon us; do you know where I can find Pedro?"

"Pedro is my husband. I am Maria. What has my Pedro done now?"

Captain Curtis smiled. "Why, nothing. Scuttlebutt at the dock says he might have an interesting story to share."

"A story?"

"You know—about the sea serpent."

Maria raised her finger. "Ahhh, yesterday I saw something very strange. I saw a pair of giant chicken feet."

Just then, Pedro drove up in his truck loaded with crates of cackling chickens.

Billy glanced at all the chickens in the crates. "I don't see any giant chickens there."

"Be quiet, Billy. Let the woman finish." The Captain rubbed his hands together in anticipation.

Pedro walked over with a crate of chickens. He smiled. "Fresh chickens, Captain." Pedro raised the crate right into the Captain's face, and a chicken nipped at the Captain's huge moustache. "Ouch!"

"Would you like a couple? Perhaps one for you and one for your friend—free of charge?"

"No, thank you, but I would like to hear the rest of Maria's story."

Maria walked over to her clothesline and pointed toward the ground. Sure enough, there were large, dried prints in the mud. "I was out hanging laundry, and the next thing I knew, I was frightened by two very large chickens. I could only see their feet behind the sheets."

Billy scratched his head. "You saw two giant chickens?"

"No! No! Just their feet."

Billy stooped down and studied the footprints in the mud. He searched through his animal book and found an emu. He nudged the Captain. "Those feet look something like an emu from Australia. Not a chicken!"

Ignoring Billy, Captain Curtis said, "It's Sissy, all right."

Maria asked, "What's an emu?"

"Never mind that. Did you see anything else, Maria?"

Pedro, paying no mind to what was going on, shouted, "How about buy one chicken, and get one half-price?"

Still ignoring Pedro, everyone watched as Maria raised her finger and pointed up. "My cat and I were far too frightened to look behind the laundry, so we climbed up the tree."

The Captain and Billy glanced up into the tree and saw that the cat was still there, frozen with fear.

"I didn't dare come down until the chicken feet were gone," Maria added.

Billy looked at the Captain, who seemed deep in thought. He turned toward the chicken tracks and the direction they were headed. The tracks led back to the ocean. Billy was more confused than ever.

Pedro lifted up his crate again and said, "How about two for twenty dollars?"

The Captain smiled. "Now *that's* a deal!" He handed Pedro the money.

Billy shook his head. "Huh?"

Back onboard the USS *Hope*, Billy and the Captain finished their dinner. Picking his teeth with a chicken feather, Captain Curtis climbed down the fish hold. "Well, First Mate, how was your first real day of dragon hunting?"

Billy, stretched out in the hammock, rubbed his shoulder, and yawned. "Captain, I'm not sure about this, and I really don't think we're gonna find a sea serpent named Sissy with emu feet."

The Captain sat on the bench, next to Davey the dive suit. "Oh, we're gonna catch her, all right. Ain't that right, Davey? But it's not the finding, Billy; it's the looking. You see, Billy, it's the voyage that's important. And even if you fail, at least it's fun looking. Ain't that right, Davey? Do you understand what I'm saying, First Mate?"

Captain Curtis heard loud snoring. He looked over at Billy, who was fast asleep. The Captain grabbed the lantern. "I guess it's just me and you, Faith. And you too, Davey."

He turned and patted the diving helmet.

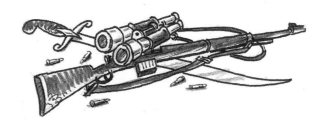

The Chase

Out of nowhere, the boat started rocking, so much so that the Captain fell back against the bulkhead and Billy was thrown out of his hammock. He cried, "What? Who? Mom!"

The Captain yelled, "All hands on deck! Emergency!"

From the pilothouse, One-Eyed Jack squawked, "Emergency! Emergency! Man your battle stations!"

The Captain bolted up the ladder and ran out onto the deck. Billy was right behind him. "It's Sissy! She's daring us into a chase!"

A wide-eyed Billy was completely baffled and a bit scared. Well, let's make that completely baffled and completely scared.

From the pilothouse, One-Eyed Jack continued to squawk, "Man your battle stations! Man your battle stations!"

Billy was running around the deck, like Pedro chasing his chickens for market. Behind him, Captain Curtis was barking out orders. "Steam, First Mate! Steam! Full steam ahead!"

Billy dashed to the engine room below and feverishly shoveled coal into the furnace. Loading the furnace to the top, he returned to the deck to see what was happening.

Captain Curtis stuck his head out of the pilothouse and yelled, "Billy! Here, take the lantern. Light the way!"

"Yes, sir!" Billy grabbed the lantern and went back on deck.

Captain Curtis shouted, "Starboard! Billy! Keep moving from side to side."

Billy ran to port.

"That's the port side! I said starboard!"

Totally mixed up, Billy continued to run back and forth. "Aye, aye, Captain!" He ran to starboard.

The Captain yelled, "Now go to the port side!"

This time, Billy went the right way.

"Good, now to starboard and then back to port side."

Billy hesitated for a moment and realized running back and forth served no purpose other than to amuse the Captain.

"Boy, you even listening?"

"Yes, sir. But make up your mind!"

The Captain stopped yelling and ran up to the bow of the boat. "I just saw Sissy's tail. Did you see it, Billy?"

"No, I didn't see anything." Billy turned his head and caught a glimpse of a fin. "Wait! Captain, I did see something."

No sooner had he said that the USS *Hope* steamed right into a bank of fog. It was so thick; it was like a snowstorm.

The Captain glanced at Billy. "Who's manning the wheel? Oh, that should be me!"

Panicked, the Captain ran back to the pilothouse and left Billy in a tizzy.

Lifting the lantern, Billy could see the faint outline of Faith, a real-life fairy, dancing in the flame. As he raised the lantern for a better look, the USS *Hope* ran hard aground.

Captain Curtis was thrown about the pilothouse, and Billy was tossed like a rag doll on the forward deck, almost falling overboard.

The Captain, holding his belly, came limping out of the pilothouse. He sighed, "Sea serpent: one; dragon hunter: zero."

From the crow's nest, One-Eyed Jack squawked, "Sea serpent: one. Dragon hunter: zero."

As the USS *Hope* settled on the white sand, the fog slowly lifted. Standing on the bow, Captain Curtis and Billy stared down at the receding tide.

Billy shook his head. "When you need a warning, where's a lighthouse when you need it, Captain?"

"Well said, Billy."

By morning, the USS *Hope* was high and dry and had left the ocean well behind.

Billy, fast asleep in the fish hold, was awakened by a tap on his shoulder. He opened his eyes and saw Davey standing over him. He rubbed his eyes; clearly, he was dreaming. Then Davey slid to the floor. Scared out of his wits, heart pounding, Billy bolted from the fish hold and went topside.

Glancing around for the Captain, he looked over the side of the boat and found him inspecting the bottom of the ship. The Captain greeted Billy, "Morning, First Mate."

"I think it's time for me to go home. Davey gives me the creeps!"

"Well, remember, Davey has spent a lot of time alone underwater. He just likes to be around people."

"Huh?"

"Just ignore him, Billy. Besides, it looks like our chase has changed from the sea to the land. It's as simple as that." The Captain climbed back onto the ship and pointed to a wide path that slithered across the barren desert. "See…Sissy has left us a trail. We're getting close to catching her. I can feel it in my salty bones."

Billy, quite worried, climbed down onto the sand. There simply was no water in sight. Billy shouted, "What about Love the dolphin? How will we find Sissy if we can't follow the dolphin?"

In a loud voice, the Captain said, "Not to worry, First Mate. Sometimes you lose Love chasing dragons, but you don't give up on Hope." The Captain patted the ship as if it were his pet dog and hurried below.

In the engine room, the Captain fiddled with the ship's gears and levers. He turned a crank round and round, and before long the ship was resting on four wheels.

Billy climbed off the boat, onto the hot sand, and stood there in amazement. Still bewildered by what he was seeing, Billy shook his head and shouted, "A ship with

wheels!"From topside, he heard One-Eyed Jack: "A ship with wheels! A ship with wheels!"

The Captain's head popped over the side, and he smiled down at Billy. "You see, Billy, the USS *Hope* isn't like any other ship."

"Yes, sir! She sure isn't!"

"That's because we have a dragon to catch! Now climb aboard—we're burning daylight."

For most of that day, the boat followed the zigzagging trail of Sissy the Sea Serpent over the hot desert sands. The boat moved up and over the hills and dunes like she was riding waves in the ocean.

Down below in the engine room, Billy shoveled the coal that made the steam boiler run. It was so hot that Billy finally took off his rain slicker.

Captain Curtis called out, "Come on up here. Get out of that heat."

Inside the pilothouse, Billy sat on a small bench and opened one of his animal books. He found the reptile section, pointed to a python, and showed the Captain. "Maybe we're just following something like this."

"Sorry to disappoint you, Billy, but pythons don't live in the desert. No, we're catchin' us a dragon…You'll see." The Captain turned to the lantern and gave it a wink.

One-Eyed Jack flew into the pilothouse and squawked, "Catchin' us a dragon… squawk! Catchin' us a dragon!"

"That's right, Jack. We're in hot pursuit, and Sissy is just over that next hill! Now, First Mate, go give the furnace another load of coal! Then come back here. We need all hands on deck."

Billy shoveled another load of coal into the boiler. He felt a tap on his shoulder, and sure enough, there was Davey, leaning against the wall. In a flash, he scrambled up the ladder and bumped into the Captain, who simply smiled.

A bit later, Billy was standing on the bow of the ship, searching the horizon through a telescope. He was still wearing only his shorts and an undershirt. He began waving frantically at the Captain in the pilothouse.

Captain Curtis stuck his head out of the pilothouse window. "You see something, First Mate?"

Billy pointed off the starboard bow. Sissy's trail led off toward what appeared to be a small clump of trees.

The Captain tooted the foghorn and turned the boat. As they moved closer, they saw a beautiful green oasis by a pool of water.

By high noon, the USS *Hope* was parked beneath a stand of shady palm trees. The ship's bow was right over the small water hole.

"I guess Sissy certainly knows her way around this desert, and she must have needed a drink.

Billy said, "She ain't the only one."

"Well, we must have just missed her. But she's close…so let's press on."

Instead, Billy grabbed the nearby life ring, tossed it down, and jumped into the water hole.

From the mast, One-Eyed Jack screamed, "Man overboard! Squawk! Man overboard!"

"I suppose a cool dip wouldn't hurt, and my clothes could use a wash." Captain Curtis leaped into the air, grabbed his knees, and shouted, "Cannonball!"

The huge tidal wave flipped Billy on his head and sent the life ring flying. The crow and Billy laughed hysterically at the Captain's antics.

Desert Bandits

By mid-afternoon, Billy was refreshed and taking a snooze beneath the palm trees. His hard work earlier in the engine room was now a distant memory.

Billy's pleasant nap was disrupted by a finger pressed to his lips. He jolted awake. "We've got company, First Mate—bad company—and it could be big trouble."

One-Eyed Jack squawked quietly. Unusual for him, he sounded like a chicken trying to lay an egg. Billy glanced at the very nervous bird.

"Who's coming?" Billy asked, slightly worried.

The Captain handed him the telescope. "Desert bandits!"

Billy looked through the glass. "I can see their dust! I see them!" Billy turned to the Captain. "How do you know they're bandits?"

"It's Hahn Kahn, a very evil dragon hunter. If he ever caught Sissy, he would use her power to find treasure. His men are all desert pirates, and we can't let them get Sissy!"

Billy, wide-eyed and frightened, said, "I really think it's time for me to go home!"

"Not to worry, Billy. I swept away our tracks. With a little luck, they may just pass us by."

Billy looked into the telescope again. It appeared that the bandits were moving away, but as he watched, they stopped and turned back toward the oasis. "No, Captain! They are headed this way!"

One-Eyed Jack squawked, "Hahn Kahn! Hahn Kahn!"

Captain Curtis grabbed the bird and tied his beak together. He took the telescope back from Billy and peeked into the glass. "Humph!" Hahn Kahn's sword was pointed straight toward the oasis. "You're right, Billy—he's leading his men this way. They must've picked up Sissy's trail."

"Looks like we're outta luck," Billy said softly.

"Are you my first mate or not?"

"Y-y-yes, sir, sir!"

"Then we'll make our own luck!"

"What? We can't outrun them in this ship?"

"Oh, yes we can!" They quickly climbed back onto the boat, and One-Eyed Jack took his place on the mast.

Within minutes, the USS *Hope* was puffing steam like a locomotive, gliding smoothly over the sand dunes.

As he peered through the telescope, Billy saw that the bandits were slowly gaining on them.

Captain Curtis stuck his head out the pilothouse door. "More steam, Billy! Get into the engine room and shovel the coal! Now!"

Billy stood at attention and saluted the Captain. "Yes, sir!"

The sweat poured off Billy's forehead as he shoveled coal like crazy. He watched the steam gauge rise and the boiler turn red hot.

Captain Curtis yelled from the pilothouse, "More coal, Billy Pip! More coal! We may not escape, but we'll give them a run for their money."

Billy's arm moved like a piston, shoveling coal into the hungry mouth of the boiler. Suddenly he stopped and yelled back, "Money! That's it! Why don't we pay off the bandits?"

The Captain laughed. "I don't have any money."

Billy yelled back, "That's because you paid twenty dollars for two *free* chickens."

The Captain added, "It doesn't matter; Hahn Kahn only wants my boat so he can catch Sissy."

One-Eyed Jack flew into the pilothouse and pecked the Captain repeatedly on the shoulder. The Captain quickly untied Jack's beak. "Get ready to fight, my feathered friend."

The Captain turned to his lantern and said, "Faith, watch over us, and keep your flame burning."

The crow left the pilothouse and flew back onto the mast, squawking like crazy. "Emergency! Emergency!"

The Captain glanced down at Davey, who was piled up in the corner of the pilothouse. "You too, Davey—get on your feet."

Billy stuck his head up through the hatch and saw Davey hanging from a hook, as though he were at attention.

Billy scrambled up the ladder into the pilothouse. He looked out the rear door and saw the bandits closing in on the USS *Hope*. "Captain, they're getting closer!"

"Billy, quick—load the cannon!"

"Cannon? We're gonna shoot the cannon?"

"Time to clean up those odds and ends that I told you about when we first met." The Captain pushed the steam throttle to its limit and began to dodge and weave in an attempt to keep the bandits from boarding.

Billy ran from the pilothouse, tripping and falling, as the ship zigzagged through the desert.

The Captain yelled, "No time for gymnastics, Billy!"

Not a second later, the bandits rode up alongside the ship.

Billy was woozy as he stood up.

The Captain yelled again, "The bow, Billy! The bow!"

Billy jumped to and made ready the cannon. "We should've had the cannon already loaded. A ready ship is a ready ship!"

The Captain stuck his head out the pilothouse door. "Bandits on the stern! Get ready to propel the boarders!"

No sooner had he given the order than six bandits jumped on deck. One-Eyed Jack swooped down, pecking fiercely at one of the bandits, who fell back overboard, hitting the ground and creating an explosion of sand. The crow flew across the deck, snatched up the paint bucket, made a quick circle, and dropped the bucket. He squawked, "Bombs away!" It hit another bandit on the head, knocking him out cold.

Billy shouted, "Good job, Jack!"

The Captain blew his air horn in agreement.

Billy grabbed a life ring and dropped it over that bandit, locking his arms by his side. The bandit tripped and fell over the side. Billy looked down and saw Davey's foot stretched out on the deck.

One-Eyed Jack screeched, "Man overboard!"

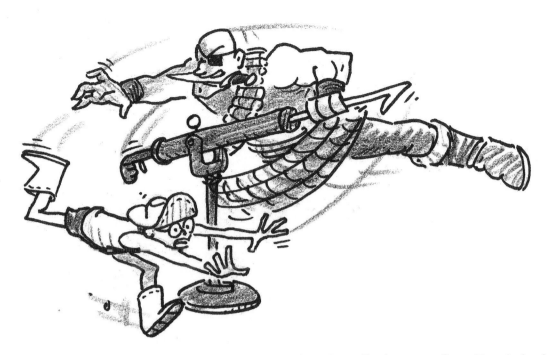

Another bandit, sword drawn, headed for the pilothouse. One-Eyed Jack planned his attack. Following him, he pecked at the man right in his backside. The bandit turned around and swung his sword at the bird but tripped over Davey's foot. Through the pilothouse door, Captain Curtis kicked him overboard.

The fourth bandit grabbed Billy, but One-Eyed Jack immediately came to his rescue. This time he latched onto the man's headband, unraveling it with his beak and spinning the bandit like a top. Through the pilothouse window, the Captain pushed the bandit, knocking him off the ship. "Man the cannon, First Mate!"

With the cannon ready, Billy waited for his orders. Faith flashed her light brightly and blinded the last two bandits as they approached.

The Captain yelled, "Fire a round over their heads, First Mate. That'll scare them away."

As Billy fumbled with the cannon, it spun around so it was aimed straight at the Captain.

Captain Curtis yelled, "Hey! Watch where you point that!"

Taking aim, Billy pulled the trigger. The harpoon's net tangled up the bandits and pulled them off the ship. As they fell, the net snagged the remaining bandits, who were still mounted on their horses.

Captain Curtis roared with laughter. "Billy Pip! I knew you would come in handy."

Not a moment later, a huge sandstorm erupted. Billy's eyes widened as he watched the Captain calmly turn the USS *Hope* directly into the path of the storm.

Billy screamed, "What are you doing?"

The Captain smiled. "This is the break I've been looking for." He grabbed Billy and jumped below decks as the massive storm engulfed the ship.

Airship

Finally, after the height of the storm had passed, Billy and Captain Curtis made sure that everyone was okay.

"Thank goodness!" said Billy. "Everyone is accounted for."

Inspecting their ship, they saw that the sandstorm had blasted off some of the USS *Hope*'s recent paint job. Squawking behind them, One-Eyed Jack appeared with the lantern in his beak.

The Captain said, "Great, I see you have Faith." The bird, spitting sand from his beak, glanced around and squawked, "Need a paint job! Need a paint job!"

Billy noticed that Davey was still in the pilothouse, standing at attention.

The Captain and Billy smiled.

Although visibility was not perfect, the Captain and Billy found no signs of the bandits. Up on the bow, the Captain lit his pipe. "I told you not to worry, First Mate."

Billy looked down at the sand. "But we lost Sissy's trail."

"Don't you see?" Captain Curtis said. "Sissy created the storm."

Billy's eyes dropped in confusion.

Captain Curtis started the engine, and the USS *Hope* slowly moved forward. Off in the distance, a gigantic stone wall loomed in front of the ship. It went on as far as the eye could see. The Captain immediately shut down the engine and joined Billy on deck.

"Sir, with that big wall in front of us, we'll never find Sissy's trail now."

"Sissy is very clever, Billy. But you can't give up. I've told you that the USS *Hope* is not like any other ship. We can get over that wall!"

Somewhat sarcastically, Billy replied, "So, she can fly in the sky, just like she glides on land and sails in the sea?"

"So, you are finally paying attention." The Captain pointed to the stern of the ship. "First Mate, open that locker."

Stuffed in the locker was an enormous canvas balloon. It took some doing, but they stretched it out on the sand and used four heavy ropes to secure it to the ship. The Captain placed a hose on one end over the ship's exhaust and inflated the canvas.

Back on deck, Billy watched the canvas inflate. The ropes holding the balloon to the ship slowly tightened. As the USS *Hope* began to rise, Billy climbed back onboard. He felt the boat rocking as though they were back on the ocean.

Billy was speechless, as the boat turned into an airship. The USS *Hope* soared over the ground, gradually rising above that very high stone wall. Billy was amazed how everything looked so different from the sky.

Captain Curtis pointed to the long, winding wall that resembled the slithering trail of a large serpent. "There's Sissy's trail! She trying to keep the chase close."

Billy grabbed his book bag, opened his world atlas, and skimmed through the pages. He found what he was looking for and showed the Captain. "Sir! That's the Great Wall of China!"

Captain Curtis nodded. "First Mate, that Great Wall will lead us to Sissy — you will see." Billy closed the book and looked at the Captain as though he were crazy.

The USS *Hope* rose higher and higher, and Billy decided to just sit back and enjoy the scenery. The fluffy clouds, fresh, cool air, and birds flying all around made for an incredible view.

"Well, First Mate, what do you think of our airship now?"

"She's an amazing boat, Captain."

"Yes, she is, First Mate."

Billy pointed toward a large dot that had appeared in the sky and was rapidly approaching the airship.

"What's that, Captain?"

"Well, clearly it's a giant bird! And it looks like it is being chased by a flock of small birds."

"Why are they chasing him?"

"They are probably protecting their nests, Billy!"

Just then, the giant bird took a nose dive and disappeared beneath the USS *Hope*.

Before they knew it, the flock of small birds landed on the ship's rigging, chirping loudly. Their chase appeared successful, and Billy wondered if they were congratulating themselves.

The Captain motioned to all the feathered hitchhikers. "They're taking a rest, Billy."

"Where are they coming from?"

"More importantly, where are they going?"

One-Eyed Jack cawed at the uninvited guests. He flapped his wings as though trying to shoo them all away. "My boat! Squawk! My boat!"

However, the birds out-numbered the crow and paid no attention to him. Disgusted and annoyed, One-Eyed Jack squawked, "Freeloaders! Freeloaders!"

The birds peeped back at the crow, as though they were laughing at him.

The Captain chuckled. "You see, Billy, those birds are protecting their nests until their young ones are old enough to fly on their own."

In a serious tone, Billy asked, "Have I left the nest yet, Captain?"

Captain Curtis smiled and lit his pipe. "What do you think, Billy?"

As they continued their journey, Billy pondered for a long time what the Captain had said. "I don't know what to think," Billy finally said, "but I know that I am getting hungry!"

A short time later, the Captain stuck his head out of the pilothouse and sniffed the air. "I smell smoke!"

"Well," Billy said, "you are smoking a pipe!"

Paying no mind to Billy, the Captain turned the ship toward a large black cloud.

"Where's there's smoke, there's fire! Where there's fire, we'll find a dragon."

"Fire and dragons? I don't like the sound of that."

The Captain lowered the airship, gradually setting her down on the edge of the forest. The Captain slowly released the air from the balloon and handed Billy the lantern. "You'll be in charge of Faith."

"Yes, sir!" Billy replied.

They headed off in search of the smoke.

They found a narrow trail that took them through pastures. The Captain and Billy came upon a young shepherd boy repairing a fence.

The Captain approached the boy. "Tell me, young man, what happened here? How did the fence get damaged?"

"Something really big crashed through and scared my sheep."

Billy noticed a hunk of bright red hair stuck to the fence post. It felt coarse in his hand as he yanked it off to show it to the Captain.

"Sissy's leaving us a clue—" The Captain's words were cut short when he sniffed the air. "Food!" He looked at Billy. "We can't hunt dragons on an empty stomach. Let's head into the village and get us some grub."

One-Eyed Jack squawked, "Empty stomach! Empty stomach!"

A short distance away, they came upon a small settlement bustling with villagers. Billy was excited by the smell of food cooking over the open wood fires.

Captain Curtis dug into his pockets and came up empty, except for the penny that Billy had given him. He looked at Billy. "By the way, do you have any more money?"

Billy turned out his empty pockets.

The Captain pointed to a huge tent surrounded by horses tied to the posts. "That's where I'll make us some money."

Billy scratched his head and followed the Captain. At the entrance, a big man stopped them and put out his hand. "Got any money? There's an admission fee."

The Captain nodded. "I have something better: I own the USS *Hope*."

Billy turned panicky. "B-but…but, sir."

From inside the tent, a voice yelled out, "Let him in! His credit is good."

The Captain, with Jack on his shoulder, entered the tent. Billy followed reluctantly. "The name's Big Red Curtis…"

"I know who you are." A large group of men were huddled around a table. A few of them stepped aside to reveal a very thin, Asian man. He had a wiry moustache, and his crooked smile revealed sparkling gold teeth.

"Hahn Kahn!"

Billy noticed that the lantern brightened for a quick moment. He took a deep, frightful breath when he recognized some of the other desert bandits. One in particular was staring right at him. Bruised, with a black eye,

43

he was the one whom Billy had chased around the cannon. The bandit didn't look happy at all.

Billy moved closer to the Captain and whispered, "Sir, I think we should go home now."

However, One-Eyed Jack perked up at the sight of the shiny coins and trinkets stacked on the card table.

The Captain took Billy's hand and placed him on a stool near the bar. He removed Billy's glasses and gave them a wipe. "Everything will be fine. Don't worry. Stay right here." The Captain leaned in and whispered, "Remember, don't move from this seat. It's very important that you don't move… and watch me clean this table out."

Billy, quite confused, could only nod.

The Captain took out his ownership papers for the USS *Hope* and handed them to the card dealer at Hahn Kahn's poker table.

In exchange, the dealer gave the Captain a bag of coins to wager with.

Billy nervously watched the Captain and Hahn Kahn trade sinister smiles. He heard the Captain say, "Funny, I don't remember you having gold teeth."

Hahn Kahn didn't answer; he only grinned.

The card game went on for over an hour, both men winning and losing. However, the Captain seemed a little luckier than Hahn Kahn, who was becoming quite suspicious of Captain Curtis's good fortune.

Every so often, the Captain looked up and could see Hahn Kahn's cards in the reflection of Billy's glasses.

Hahn Kahn wondered why the Captain had so much interest in the boy. His eyes narrowed as he watched the Captain play his next hand.

Meanwhile, with no one paying attention to him, One-Eyed Jack was busy looting the tent, stuffing his bag with anything shiny he could find.

Obeying the Captain's orders, Billy stayed glued to the bar seat. However, the bandit whom Billy had shot overboard came toward him and slapped him on the back, knocking off his glasses. "Nice to see you again, kid!"

Captain Curtis realized Billy had slipped off his stool and lost his glasses.

"Time out!" he shouted. "My first mate needs me."

A bit suspicious, Hahn Kahn noticed the Captain rushing off to help Billy.

The Captain could see that Billy was very nervous and whispered, "How you doing, kid? Are you okay, son?"

Billy gave him a half-smile and said, "I'm awful queasy, sir. I need to go home now."

The Captain laughed. "It's just your nerves, boy!"

Billy nodded. "Is there something funny about my glasses?"

"Never mind 'bout that. Now pay attention, and don't move from this seat." Again, the Captain positioned Billy just right, but when he turned around, Hahn had switched places with him.

Hahn Kahn grinned. "Is there a problem, Captain Curtis?"

"Not at all! Let's play cards."

Hahn Kahn glanced over at Billy. "Interesting—the view is much better from here." Obviously, Hahn Kahn could see the Captain's cards, just as the Captain had seen his.

As the game came to an end, there was a pile of coins and the USS *Hope*'s papers in the middle of the table. At this point in the game, it didn't appear that Captain Curtis was doing very well.

Billy knew from Hahn Kahn's sinister grin that Captain Curtis was in deep trouble. Kahn was beating the Captain at his own game.

The bandits moved closer to the table, waiting for the Captain to play his last hand.

Captain Curtis laid down his hand. Hahn Kahn grinned, and his gold teeth glistened. "The ship is mine!"

The bandits shouted victory. The Captain jumped up and flipped over the table. A wild fight started, and the Captain tossed punches in every direction. The bandits dove to the floor, trying to grab the money.

The sounds of the coins rolling on the floor made One-Eyed Jack squawk. The crow quickly scooped up some coins in his beak, tucking them into the pouch under his wing.

Captain Curtis almost stepped on the bird as he and Hahn Kahn dashed to the ground for the ship's papers. Hahn Kahn beat the Captain out and snapped up the papers. Hahn Kahn was the new owner of the USS *Hope*.

The bandit, the one Billy feared most, yanked out his sword and approached the bar. One-Eyed Jack dove at the man's ankle, and he tripped. He fell down right in front of Billy, who threw up all over him. "Gee, sorry about that, Mr. Bandit."

"Nice job, First Mate!" The Captain glanced at Jack and shouted, "Keep them busy!"

One-Eyed Jack zoomed around like a black hornet, attacking the bandits.

As they passed the main pole holding up the tent, the Captain gave it a swift kick. The tent collapsed just as they cleared the entrance.

But they weren't safe for long.

Captain Curtis and Billy, with no food, and no Sissy, were still being pursued by a gang of very angry bandits. Even with One-Eyed Jack and Faith guiding them through the forest, everything seemed hopeless.

The Cave

Captain Curtis and Billy scrambled and tripped as they made their way back through the woods. They didn't stop until they reached the base of a small mountain overgrown like a jungle.

One-Eyed Jack returned from scouting the terrain and landed on the Captain's shoulder. With his wing, the crow pointed to a hidden cave. Steam poured from the mouth of the cave, and together with jagged hanging rocks, it resembled the mouth of a horned-dragon.

"Well done, Jack. I suspect this could be Sissy's hideout."

"Do you smell that smoke?"

While the bird nodded vigorously, Billy just shook his head. "We aren't actually going in there... Are we? It looks far too dangerous!"

Behind them, they could hear the angry bandits approaching.

"Well, First Mate, follow me or end up in the hands of Hahn Kahn!"

"But, Captain, we don't have Love or Hope! We're doomed!"

The Captain raised the lantern. "Never underestimate the power of Faith. As long as she lights the way, nothing can harm us."

Without hesitating, One-Eyed Jack took off and flew into the cave. Captain Curtis grabbed Billy's hand and followed the crow.

Despite Faith's light, the cave was black as ink, and they felt a cool mist flowing through the cavern. They heard the soft drips of water falling from the ceiling onto the rocky floor.

They splashed through puddles as they went deeper into the maze of tunnels.

Billy whispered, "Which way?"

"Let Faith light the way," the Captain replied.

The lantern brightened considerably, revealing the rocky surroundings. As they continued to move deeper into the cave, they could see something glowing in the distance. Billy and the Captain immediately stopped in their tracks.

Billy pointed. "What's that, Captain?"

One-Eyed Jack squawked, "What's that? What's that?"

"Good question, First Mate. Let's find out, why don't we, Jack?" The crow took off toward the strange prism of color.

As they followed the crow, they could hear One-Eyed Jack squawking like an Irish leprechaun, "Pots of gold! Squawk! Pots of gold!"

Billy and the Captain rushed toward the glow and were soon overwhelmed by the sight. The chamber was filled with gold coins, silver pieces, gems, and diamonds. One-Eyed Jack was one very excited bird; his black feathers were standing on end as if he had been electrocuted.

"Shhhhh, Jack! Quiet!"

One-Eyed Jack, overcome by the sight of the treasure, passed out on a pile of sparkling diamonds.

The Captain glanced down at the crow. "Well, I guess that's one way of keeping him quiet."

Billy reached for some of the treasure, but the Captain grabbed his arm.

"Don't touch anything! This all belongs to Sissy. I suspect she's been collecting this pirate booty from sunken ships for a long time. Now you know why Hahn Kahn wants Sissy."

Billy nodded, but he was astounded by the riches. "Wow!" he whispered. "Pirate treasure! Let's help ourselves."

"No! You don't take what isn't earned."

For a long moment, Billy stared at the Captain, his eyeglasses slightly tilted.

"Wait a second! What about that card game with Hahn Kahn?"

"Look, son, I admire your position, but I was earning that money to buy food."

"You were cheating! That doesn't make it right."

"Well said, First Mate. It's not right—a good lesson learned."

One-Eyed Jack slowly came to. Looking around, he slipped a diamond into his pouch. Faith's light brightened and then dimmed, as though she were sending out a warning.

Suddenly, the cave trembled as if a small earthquake had hit.

The Captain turned to the crow. "Jack! Put the diamond back!"

The crow squawked and dropped it back into the pile.

They could hear the oncoming desert bandits, screaming and yelling as if they were being chased by something.

"What's going on, Captain?"

The Captain placed his finger to Billy's lips. "Sissy just gave us a warning. We gotta move quickly. We don't want to be on the wrong end of that dragon. 'Specially when she's chasin' bandits who want to steal her treasure."

The Captain and Billy quickly headed away from the approaching commotion.

Moments later, the desert bandits entered the treasure room, and they, too, stopped in their tracks. They were so shocked and overwhelmed by the sight that their eyes glowed with greed. "We're rich! We're rich!" they shouted.

Soon after those words were spoken, the cavern began to shake again. The walls and floor cracked open, and rocks fell from the ceiling. Some of the treasure even tumbled through the cracks and disappeared.

Without even a coin, the bandits fled for their lives.

******

The Captain and Billy ran faster as the wind roared from behind them. It sounded like they were being chased by a train. The blast of wind blew out Faith's flame and knocked the lantern out of the Captain's hands. In the pitch darkness, Billy, struggling with his book bag, walked blindly forward.

Completely alone, Billy could hear his heart thumping in his chest, as he tried to decide which way to go. Suddenly, a pair of glowing red eyes watched Billy for a moment and then disappeared into the darkness.

Billy heard the Captain shout, "First Mate! Where are you, boy?"

Whispering, Billy responded, "Captain…over here…I'm here! Here! Over here!" He glanced once more at the eyes and started running toward the sound of the Captain's voice. He could now see the light at the mouth of the cavern.

Just as Billy was about to reach the Captain, a giant fireball shot forward. The blast lifted him off his feet and tossed him through the air like a human cannonball.

The Captain reached out and caught Billy before he was thrown off the cliff into the harbor below.

Billy looked up at Captain Curtis and said, "What was that?" The Captain replied, "Sissy was warning those bandits. Did you see her in there?"

"I'm not sure what I saw. But I'm not going back in there to find out."

Captain Curtis held up the lantern. "Maybe we didn't catch Sissy, but we found Faith again." He pointed toward the harbor. "And when you have Faith, Hope will follow."

Worried, Billy searched the harbor, but he didn't see anything.

"How are we going to get Hope—I mean, your ship—back? I can't go home unless we have the ship."

The Captain removed his spyglass from his belt and searched the horizon.

"Well, I may not see Hope, but right now, I see something that might help us."

The Match

As Captain Curtis and Billy continued on their journey, Billy was excited to see a large, bustling city not too far away. At the city's edge, the Captain pointed to a colorful banner blowing in the wind. "That's it! Come on, Billy, let's go."

It wasn't long before Billy's stomach was growling. The aroma of food filled the air, and as they made their way through the crowded streets, Billy couldn't believe his eyes. He saw livestock of every kind and ripe, delicious fruits and vegetables. "Captain, I'm so hungry."

The Captain replied, "We'll eat soon, but we have business to attend to."

Wondering what was next, Billy mumbled, "Here we go again!"

Billy heard yelling coming from a large, open courtyard just past the marketplace. People were gathered around a ring, watching some kind of sporting event. To Billy, it was apparent that something big was going on.

Billy was shocked to see a man being tossed through the air. The man crashed into the onlookers and created a loud ruckus. "Captain, did you see that? What's going on?" Billy could hardly control his excitement.

Captain Curtis nodded, and he turned to Billy. "You see, son, it's a wrestling match!"

Billy saw the wrestlers lining up around the ring. Most of them were smaller than the Captain. He noticed that people in the crowd were giving money to an old woman inside a booth.

As the Captain moved closer to the booth and the line of wrestlers waiting their turn, he said, "First place the bets, and I'll do the rest."

Billy stopped walking. "We have no money, Captain."

The Captain paused for a moment, realizing that Billy was right.

Both of them glanced at One-Eyed Jack, perched on the Captain's shoulder. The Captain smiled at Billy.

The crow squawked in disagreement, "Not my pearl! Squawk! Not my pearl!"

Moments later, Billy approached the old woman who was seated behind a table in the betting shack. She had no teeth and a rather sharp nose. Her white hair was braided and tied up in a bun. She resembled the old witches Billy had read about.

Billy handed her the pearl from Jack's eye. She mumbled something, but Billy couldn't understand her. She rolled the pearl around in her hand and examined it with a magnifying glass.

Sitting on the Captain's shoulder, Jack quietly watched the old woman as she studied his pearl. Like a pirate from *Treasure Island*, One-Eyed Jack was now sporting an eye patch.

The crow squawked, "Careful with that! Careful with that!"

She weighed the pearl and shook her head. "Not much value here."

One-Eyed Jack squawked loudly, clearly in disagreement.

The woman glanced up at Captain Curtis and asked, "Name?"

"Curtis."

She wrote the Captain's name on a slip of paper and handed Billy his ticket. The Captain was now entered into the wrestling match.

The Captain wasted no time getting ready for the match. He removed his cap and jacket, and Jack flew onto Billy's shoulder. Like a true showman, the Captain strolled around the ring, flexing his muscles. The crowd both clapped and booed. The Captain smiled as he bowed and wiggled his hips from side to side. The crowd went crazy!

"Let's get ready to crumble!" squawked Jack.

Billy glanced at the crow and said, "I sure hope the Captain knows what he's doing."

The referee entered the ring and pointed up to the betting board. "Curtis versus Lee," he shouted. As Lee entered the ring, Billy noticed he wasn't very big; in fact, he didn't look very tough either.

Captain Curtis leaned over to Billy. "See, I told you there was nothing to worry about."

At the sound of the bell, the Captain returned to the middle of the ring to meet his first opponent. They hadn't even shook hands when Lee caught the Captain off guard and tripped him. The Captain tumbled to the ground, and the crowd roared.

Billy ran to the edge of the ring. "Aren't you supposed to win, Captain?"

He gave Billy a sly smile. "I meant to do that. It's all part of my plan."

The Captain took a few more tumbles at the hands of his opponent and smiled to himself. "Now it's my turn." With one swift move, the Captain pinned Lee to the ground, and the referee counted, "One…two…three…!"

Lifting the Captain's arm, the referee shouted, "We have a winner!"

Captain Curtis's name moved up a notch on the winners' board.

Billy wasted no time collecting their winnings from the old hag. With his hat full of money, Billy ran back to the Captain's corner. "We did it, Captain. Now we can buy back the ship."

Captain Curtis laughed. "That won't even buy dinner. You see, Hahn Kahn has waited a long time for my ship, and he ain't gonna give it up cheap. You just keep bettin', and I'll just keep winnin'." The Captain stood up, cracked his knuckles, and said, "Like taking candy from a baby!"

Billy reluctantly went back and placed another bet.

Just then, the next competitor entered the ring.

The Captain stood there and looked over at the referee, who was staring up at the board. Captain Curtis lifted three fingers into the air and yelled, "I'll take on three men at once."

The audience gasped. Even the old hag was impressed.

Billy shook his head, and One-Eyed Jack squawked loudly.

Once the three men were in the ring, they began flexing their muscles and showing off.

The crowd roared with excitement, and a betting frenzy began. Billy and Jack were both worried.

At the beginning of the match, the Captain played the crowd, letting his opponents get the better of him. In the next round, the Captain demonstrated his amazing strength and simply tossed them all out of the ring, one-two-three.

Billy rushed to collect their winnings and broke into a smile. "Maybe it *is* like taking candy from a baby."

The old woman grunted at Billy.

A hush fell over the crowd, and Billy turned around. Towering above everyone in the audience was the largest man Billy had ever seen. As the crowd stepped aside, Billy's heart began to pound as he saw Hahn Kahn leading this giant toward the ring.

Shocked at the man's bulging muscles and enormous feet, Billy couldn't take his eyes off the giant. He swallowed hard at the sight of the monster wrestler.

Even One-Eyed Jack peeped like a baby bird begging for a worm.

Hahn Kahn said, "Well, Captain, I suppose you want your boat back."

"That's the plan."

"Beat my giant, and it's all yours."

"I think we should leave…while you're still in one piece!" said Billy. His comment made the crowd laugh and even brought a crooked grin to Hahn Kahn's lips.

Captain Curtis quickly responded, "The bigger they are, First Mate, the harder they fall."

One-Eyed Jack squawked, "Harder they fall! Harder they fall!"

Hahn Kahn approached Billy. "Well, boy, how much money do you have?"

Billy showed him his hat full of money.

Hahn Kahn grinned. "Not much! But I'll take the bet, because the Captain's luck is about to run out. And I'm glad I'm here to see it."

From the corner of the ring, the Captain winked at Billy.

Billy nodded and turned to Hahn Kahn. "We have a bet, sir!" They both spit into their hands and shook.

Hahn Kahn handed the ship's papers to the old hag, and Billy handed over their money.

As the giant entered the ring, his footsteps sounded like tree trunks crashing to the ground. The Captain's eyes widened and a look of fear crossed his face.

As they waited for the round to begin, the Captain and the giant just stared at each other.

Hahn Kahn took a seat right alongside Billy, and his bandits settled in around them. The bell rang, signaling the first round.

The giant, like an enormous mountain, moved slowly around the ring, growling at the Captain.

Without waiting, the Captain punched the giant's belly. It was like hitting a brick wall. Annoyed, the giant grabbed the Captain by the arms and tossed him to the ground.

Again and again, the giant bounced the Captain's body around like a basketball. Every time the Captain tried to get up, the laughing giant slammed him back down.

One-Eyed Jack squawked, "Harder they fall! Harder they fall!"

Billy tried to get up from his seat, but Hahn Kahn placed his hand on his shoulder and sat him back down. "It'll all be over soon."

Still on the ground, Captain Curtis nodded to Billy. "It's all part of the plan."

For some reason, Billy didn't believe him this time.

Trying to help the Captain, Billy tossed him his copy of *Treasure Island*. The Captain grabbed the hard-cover novel and whacked the giant in the nose. For the first time, the giant wobbled and fell to one knee. Regaining his balance, he threw a wicked punch, but the Captain, using the book, blocked the giant's hand.

The Captain handed the novel back to Billy and said, "That certainly came in handy. I guess being a bookworm is kinda cool!"

"Time out!" Hahn Kahn stood and approached the giant. "Let me take a look at that hand." While he inspected the giant's hand, Kahn slipped him a handful of black pepper.

At the start of round two, the giant blew the pepper at the Captain.

Blinded, the Captain began to sneeze wildly. The giant, wasting no time, grabbed Captain Curtis and lifted him over his head. Showing off, he spun the Captain around and slammed him to the ground.

One-Eyed Jack squawked loudly, "Game over! Game over!"

Hahn Kahn said to Billy, "I know you want to go home. Why don't you throw in the towel, and I'll see that you get there?"

The Captain looked at his injured shoulder and then over at Billy.

"This match isn't over as long as I have my first mate."

"Kahn shouted, "Your first mate can't finish this match; he can't beat this giant."

Captain Curtis raised his finger into the air and said in a blustery tone, "Billy Pip is a *faithful* dragon-hunting, bandit-dodging, adventure-seeking, fearless sailor of the seven seas."

Billy did a double take at that comment and unexpectedly puffed out his chest in agreement. This made Captain Curtis quite proud.

The Captain looked at Hahn Kahn and added, "If my first mate beats the giant, we get the USS *Hope* back, and you can even keep our money."

"And when he loses?"

"You keep the ship and all the winnings, and I vow never to hunt dragons again."

Billy's eyes grew bigger than his glasses.

Kahn rubbed his chin. He clearly liked the terms of the Captain's wager. "Never hunt dragons again?"

"Not one salty scale!"

The Captain and Hahn Kahn both spit into their hands and shook. "We have a deal!"

The Captain looked over at the old hag and said, "The name is Pip! Billy Pip!"

Billy Pip fainted when he saw his name go up on the board. Everyone laughed; even Hahn Kahn had a hard time controlling himself.

In an effort to wake him, One-Eyed Jack poured water on the boy's face. The crow squawked, "Man overboard! Man overboard!"

Everyone laughed.

The Captain, with his arm in a sling, stood over Billy as he came to. Billy whispered, "I really want to go home."

Captain Curtis shook his head. "We can't! Not without the USS *Hope*."

"But he's a giant! A real giant!"

"Now listen up, First Mate: the bigger they are, the harder they fall."

One-Eyed Jack was about to squawk in disagreement, when the Captain grabbed him and held his beak together.

"Not to worry, Billy. The fear inside you will give you the strength you need."

59

"That's what you think, sir!" The roar of the crowd drowned out Billy's words. The man rang the bell, and the audience turned silent. The only sound Billy could hear was that of his own heart thumping out of his chest.

The giant moved slowly toward Billy, and the crowd gasped. The giant stopped, looked around at the audience, and lurched toward Billy. Without hesitation, Billy ran around the ring like Pedro's chickens trying to escape.

The crowd roared with laughter as Billy scampered back and forth while the giant tried to catch him. Finally the giant grew tired and threw up his arms in frustration.

Captain Curtis yelled to the referee, "Time out!" He leaned inside the ring and whispered, "I'm very proud of you, Billy. You've done a great job so far."

Billy shook his head. "Are you watching the same match? He's a mountain!"

"Billy, don't you see? That's your real problem. You're always relying on your sight instead of your heart." The Captain removed Billy's eyeglasses and sent him back into the ring. "Now go beat that giant! He's out of breath and ready to fall." The Captain turned to One-Eyed Jack. "He's gonna do it."

In clear disagreement, One-Eyed Jack shook his head from side to side.

Inside the ring, Billy was blind without his glasses. He yelled, "I can't see!"

"That's the idea, Billy. If you can't see him, you can't fear him."

Billy ran screaming toward the giant, who stood there and laughed. Billy dropped his head and rammed the giant square in the stomach. The giant dropped to his knees.

The Captain yelled, "That's using your head, kid!"

At the same time, a strange gust of green-and-blue wind spiraled through the crowd, knocking off hats and snapping flags from their poles. The Captain looked up at the rooftops, knowing something the others didn't.

At the top of the tallest building, someone or something was watching the match.

The crowd cheered for Billy, while up on the roof a loud purr went unheard by the audience below.

It took a minute, but the giant finally stood up. In an attempt to confuse the giant, Billy ran around the ring a few more times. The crowd laughed and cheered for Billy Pip.

Suddenly, like a wild monkey, Billy scooted up the giant's back and grabbed onto his big head. He wrapped his legs around the giant's neck and covered the giant's eyes with his hands. Billy was riding the giant like a rodeo bull.

Enjoying the antics, the crowd screamed, but their laughter only angered the giant. Hahn Kahn yelled, "He's only a boy! Get this over with!"

The giant reached up and grabbed Billy's arms and tossed him to the ground, knocking the wind out of him.

The Captain shouted, "Pip. Pip. Pip."

The crowd followed the captain's lead, gradually getting louder and louder. "Pip! Pip! Pip!"

Captain Curtis had secretly placed Faith the lantern on the edge of the ring, close to Billy.

Faith flashed, and Billy saw the giant's boots reflected in the lantern. With a spark of determination, Billy realized, *I gotta beat him. I want to go home!*

Still on the ground behind the giant, Billy rolled over and cleverly managed to tie the giant's bootlaces together. Billy jumped up, stuck his tongue out at the giant, and ran away.

Ringside, Hahn Kahn shouted, "Get him! Finish this!"

When the giant tried to grab Billy, he lost his balance, and, like a towering oak tree, he fell and knocked himself out.

For a moment, the audience fell silent. Hahn Kahn was stunned and in disbelief.

Without hesitation, Billy placed his foot on the giant's chest. He had won the match!

The audience erupted into cheers. "Pip! Pip! Pip!"

The referee grabbed Billy's hand and raised it over his head. "We have a winner!"

Captain Curtis lifted Billy onto his shoulder and handed him his eyeglasses. Together they

shouted, "The bigger they are, the harder they fall!"

One-Eyed Jack squawked, "Billy: one! Giant: zero!"

Meanwhile, the crowd continued to chant, "Pip! Pip! Pip!"

Billy smiled from ear to ear, enjoying all the attention.

Another strange blast of wind zipped through the crowd and disappeared.

Hahn Kahn looked angry as he collected his share of the winnings from the old hag. The Captain took back the USS *Hope*'s papers, and One-Eyed Jack got his pearl.

The Captain and Billy enjoyed a nice dinner onboard the ship. Love found her way back having splashed happily by their side.

"Everyone is celebrating your victory, Billy, even Love," the Captain said, as he lit his pipe. "I knew Love would find us again."

Billy yawned and stretched.

"You better get to bed," the Captain added. "We've got a big day tomorrow."

"You mean we're finally going home? I've been meaning to tell you; I really, really miss my mom."

"I understand how you feel, son. We'll see her soon—I promise. But we can't go home yet—we've got Faith, Love, and Hope together again, and they're on our side. Tomorrow it's full steam ahead, and I'm gonna need your help."

Billy, feeling homesick, silently left the galley. He climbed down into the fish hold and went to bed.

Later, the Captain checked in on Billy, who was fast asleep. He leaned in and whispered, "Don't worry, son, you'll see your mother soon."

Under the Ice

Billy woke up freezing. His teeth were chattering, and he was so cold that he could see his breath. He wondered, *what has the Captain done now?*

He climbed out of the fish hold and suddenly wished he had a warmer coat. Everywhere he looked were icebergs as far as the eye could see. Billy noticed that the ship's riggings were blanketed with a layer of ice. He thought the USS *Hope* looked like a cake covered in frosting.

He hurried into the pilothouse, where he found the Captain, pencil in hand, leaning over a chart, checking the ship's course.

Billy stared out the pilothouse window and shook his head. "What's going on? We're not moving. Where are we? And why is it so cold?"

"We're stuck in the ice."

"Stuck?" Billy's voice turned worrisome. "Stuck? Stuck where?"

The Captain replied, "At the top of the map. Have you ever heard of the Arctic?"

"Yes, I've seen it in my atlas many times."

"Well, First Mate, we're not quite there, despite the cold weather. But you'll find the people are warm and friendly."

Billy said, "This place doesn't look very warm and friendly. I wish I was going home instead. I'm cold, I'm hungry, we're running out of food, and I'm tired of searching the world for something that doesn't exist."

"Look, son, Love was right on Sissy's trail, and we should catch up to that dragon as soon as the ice breaks. Of course, that could take some time."

Billy shook his head in frustration. "I think we need to talk, Captain." In a stern voice, he said, "Sir, Love is not a mermaid; she's a dolphin. And Faith isn't a fairy; it's a lantern. Hope is a magical ship, but after all, she's just a boat. And another thing, according to everything I know: there's no animal that has giant chicken feet, red hair, and fish scales. Sissy simply doesn't exist! It's all in your head!"

Billy, waiting patiently for a reply, watched the Captain as he calmly lit his pipe. The Captain remained silent for a long time.

Finally, the Captain replied, "Well, Billy, if it's all in my head, then what made the tracks around this 'boat'?"

Billy's expression turned to shock. They both left the pilothouse and peered over the port side of the ship. Lo and behold, in the snow-covered ice they saw giant tracks that circled the boat.

Billy searched his encyclopedia, shook his head, and whispered, "It can't be. This place is far too cold for an ostrich or an emu. What is going on?"

"Well, First Mate, those tracks don't belong to an ostrich or an emu. They belong to a sea serpent named Sissy!"

"Sea serpent! Sea serpent!" Jack squawked.

"But? But?"

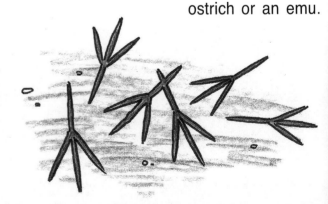

66

The Captain hung a rope ladder over the side. "No buts 'bout it. Come on, Billy, we're going hunting."

The Captain, One-Eyed Jack, and Billy, carrying the lantern, climbed down onto the ice. As they headed away from the ship, the ice creaked beneath their feet.

Billy asked the Captain, "Is the ice safe?"

The Captain replied, "Well, it is no more dangerous than anything else we've done so far!"

Billy looked at the Captain and rolled his eyes. "Well, that makes me feel a whole lot better…*not*!"

They followed the tracks for what seemed like miles, and they came upon a small village nestled in the hillside.

Captain Curtis said, "We're finally going to find Sissy. We're almost at the end of our journey, Billy."

They noticed that the tracks stopped suddenly.

"Where did Sissy go, Captain?"

Captain Curtis glanced up at the sky. "She's a smart one, that Sissy."

"How will we find her now?"

The Captain ignored Billy's question and focused on the dozens of igloos a hundred yards ahead. The Captain sniffed the air and said, "I smell fish! And we can't hunt dragons on an empty stomach. Let's go!"

Billy thought of his mother's spaghetti and meatballs and her yummy chocolate cake. He felt truly homesick and mumbled to himself, "Not fish again."

The villagers seemed very happy to see Captain Curtis. It was obvious that he had been there before.

"They seem to know you, Captain."

"Well, son, I do get 'round hunting dragons."

The Captain still had a hard time squeezing through the entrance of even the largest igloo in the village.

Inside, the Elder Chief was seated on a rug of soft animal skins. He looked at the Captain and smiled a toothless grin. "Good to see you again, Red Bear."

Billy laughed. "Red Bear?"

One-Eyed Jack squawked, "Red Bear! Red Bear!"

The Captain chuckled along with everyone else. "You should hear what they call me in Africa."

The Elder motioned for everyone to sit down. "Come, Red Bear—we've been expecting you. It's time for supper. Tonight we have blubber soup. Every night we have blubber soup."

"My favorite!" the Captain replied.

Billy's eyes widened at the Elder's comment. He was happy that it wasn't fish, but he wasn't too sure what blubber soup tasted like.

The village women entered carrying pots of steaming soup. As hungry as he was, Billy's mouth dropped when he saw a young Eskimo girl enter the igloo.

Noticing Billy's reaction, the Elder said, "This is my granddaughter, Ekia."

While they ate, Billy and Ekia kept looking at each other. Billy was quite shy, but Ekia was playful and giggled with the other girls.

When they finished their supper, the Elder Chief told the children to go play outside. Ekia took Billy's hand and led him outside while the adults stayed behind to talk.

The Captain appeared quite proud as he watched Billy and Ekia leave the igloo. The Elder studied the Captain's reaction to Billy. "Fine boy!"

Captain Curtis nodded. "We've been on many adventures together. He is learning much about the world."

"That is good, Red Bear! Who better than you to teach him?" With that, the Captain and the Elder roared with laughter.

As night fell, the igloos were all lit up by their oil lamps. The small flames danced about the village, creating beautiful, snowy shadows.

On the same field as a herd of caribou, the children were having a good time kicking around a leather ball. Billy was chasing Ekia, who fell to the ground, laughing.

Ekia turned and looked at Billy, whose eyes dropped shyly. She asked, "Why are you here, Billy?"

"Well, crazy Captain Curtis is hunting a make-believe dragon named Sissy…a sea monster or something."

"A sea monster?"

"Yeah, real crazy, huh?"

"It's not crazy to follow what you believe. My grandfather says that you can only find that which you believe."

Billy pointed to the Captain, who appeared to be gesturing to the villagers and entertaining them with funny stories.

"But he's crazy! Look at him—he's talking to a lantern."

However, Ekia seemed to know something that Billy didn't. They sat on the ground for a few moments, watching a husky puppy named Hoku play in the snow.

One of the children kicked the ball into the herd of caribou, and Hoku quickly ran after the ball. Ekia yelled, "Hoku! Come back here! You'll scare the herd."

However, the puppy paid no attention to her.

Billy said, "Don't worry. I'll get him!" As Billy approached the herd, he found them snorting and scratching their hooves on the frozen ground.

Billy stooped down to look for the puppy, but was shocked at what he saw. Among the herd of caribou was a pair of giant chicken feet. It was an incredible sight.

He snapped off his glasses and wiped away the foggy dew. When he put them back on, he saw those same red eyes he had seen in the cave. He gasped and tumbled backward. It was Sissy!

Not a second later, Sissy disappeared into a swirling tornado of wind and snow. *It can't be!* Billy thought.

Hoku, following after the swirling snow, ran right to the water's edge and fell through the ice. The dog struggled as he tried to stay afloat.

Without any fear, Billy bolted toward the ice. However, a big hand grabbed him and lifted him off the ground. He turned and saw the worried expression on the Captain's face. "You can't go out there, Billy. It's far too dangerous." Captain Curtis placed his hand on the boy's shoulder.

One-Eyed Jack and the villagers all turned quiet and somber. Billy stared at the Captain in utter disbelief.

Ekia rested her head against her grandfather and started to cry.

Hearing Ekia's sobs, Billy, unafraid of the danger, ran out onto the ice. But the ice gave away, and with a loud crack, Billy felll through.

Without thinking, Captain Curtis rushed after Billy, but he was far too heavy, and the ice began to give way. He knew he needed to get to the ship.

The Captain, carrying Faith, and One-Eyed Jack on his shoulder, hopped bravely from ice floe to ice floe, heading for the USS *Hope*.

When he finally reached the ship, he was exhausted. He pulled his tired and heavy body over the side and plopped onto the deck.

Searching for Davey, Captain Curtis screamed, "This is not the time for hide-and-seek, Davey! Come out; come out, wherever you are!" The locker door in the pilothouse sprung open, and there stood Davey at full attention.

On the Captain's orders, One-Eyed Jack flew to the spot where Billy had fallen through the ice. He circled overhead and squawked, "Man overboard! Man overboard!"

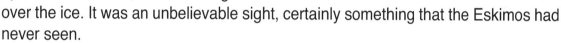

Meanwhile, on the water's edge, the villagers had tied long poles together and were hopelessly trying to reach the spot where Billy and Hoku had gone through the ice. In the distance they could hear a horn tooting. The USS *Hope*, up on her wheels, came rolling over the ice. It was an unbelievable sight, certainly something that the Eskimos had never seen.

On the deck of the USS *Hope*, Captain Curtis struggled to put on the dive suit. While he bounced around on one leg, he yelled, "I promise I'll go on a diet if you just let me…" He tripped on the dangling air hose, and the dive helmet fell and bumped the lantern.

Both Davey's helmet and Faith plunged into the icy water.

A moment later, Hoku floated in against the boat. He was sitting inside Billy's hat. It had acted like a raft and saved the puppy.

Captain Curtis shouted, "Well, I'll be…" Then, in desperation, he yelled, "Faith, go find our boy! Go find our boy!"

Showdown

Treading in the icy water, Billy felt his lips turning numb. Just as he started to sink under the ice, he was surprised to find both Love and Faith, both very real, right there with him. The mermaid wrapped her arms around Billy and gave him a big smooch.

Onboard the USS *Hope*, Captain Curtis opened the pressure gauges and released air into the dive helmet.

Guided by the glow of Faith's lantern, Love lifted the boy and managed to get him into the floating dive helmet, where he was able to breathe again.

Billy smiled at them both and said, "I'm sorry I didn't see you before."

Love laughed. "Sometimes, Billy, it's hard to see what you don't believe."

"I feel like a fool," Billy said.

Faith smiled and happily flapped her Fairy wings, "Aren't we all a little foolish now and then? We better get you topside before the Captain comes down here after you."

Love slowly guided them toward the surface.

Leaning over the side and peering through his spyglass, Captain Curtis could see air bubbles rising.

The Captain yelled, "Billy's gonna be okay! He found Faith and Love!"

One-Eyed Jack squawked, "Faith and Love! Faith and Love!"

Without warning, the USS *Hope* rocked and heaved. The drifting ice floes shifted and pressed the air hose against the ship's hull, stopping the flow of oxygen and leaving Billy gasping for air.

Captain Curtis immediately realized what had happened.

He grabbed a sledgehammer and climbed down onto the ice. Trying to bust a hole in the ice, he swung the hammer so hard that he broke the handle.

Now Billy was right up against the ice floe, and he could see the Captain standing there helpless, holding the broken hammer.

Captain Curtis glanced up at the sky

and removed his cap. "We need some help! I can't let anything happen to my first mate!"

Moments later, the Captain's prayers were answered, but not in the way he expected. A massive fireball dropped from above, and the Captain and the villagers on the shore jumped for cover. Even One-Eyed Jack flew away. The fireball melted through the ice, like a hot knife to butter.

Billy watched in awe as Sissy swam all around him. For the first time, he saw that she was indeed a rare creature. Just as the Captain had described, she had shark fins, fish scales, red hair, antlers, and, of course, those chicken-like feet. However, the Captain had never mentioned her warm and friendly face, and as sea serpents went, she wasn't very scary. In fact, Billy thought she was rather pretty.

Faith said, "Billy, don't worry—Sissy is harmless. Hold out your hand."

Billy quickly reached out and took hold of her red mane and climbed aboard. Sissy rushed to the surface and delivered Billy to safety.

Once above the water, Sissy continued up into the sky, creating an enormous wave of water that rained down on everyone in the village.

Sissy made a couple of quick loops above the village and then shot straight up toward the heavens.

Ekia hugged her grandfather.

Below, Jack, Faith, and Love watched in pure amazement.

The Captain was thrilled to see Billy riding on the backside of Sissy. "Betcha that boy is having the ride of his life!"

One-Eyed Jack squawked, "Joy-ride! Joy-ride!"

As he hung on to Sissy's antlers, Billy felt like a rodeo cowboy. He was thrilled, but more than anything else, he wasn't scared at all.

Billy wondered what his mother would think if she could see him now.

Sissy knew that Billy was enjoying himself, so she flew higher and faster, giving him a heart-pounding ride. The boy loved every second. It was indeed a magical trip.

The momentum created a rainbow that painted the heavens and lit up the sky.

From the ground, Captain Curtis and One-Eyed Jack watched Sissy weave her incredible colors around the aurora borealis.

Captain Curtis said, "Yes, sir, the northern lights have never looked as wonderful as they do tonight." The Captain couldn't help but smile proudly.

One-Eyed Jack squawked, "Billy Pip! Billy Pip!"

The Elder Chief added, "Every time the dragon returns, the magic lights turn brighter than before."

Billy was enjoying the greatest show on Earth: the northern lights, aurora borealis! He had the Captain to thank for all of this. He also realized that Ekia was right: Captain Curtis wasn't crazy; he was truly a great man.

Billy couldn't have been happier, although he did wish that his mother could have been there to share in this adventure. He was so proud to call the Captain his friend; he would make sure that his mother met him.

In the distance, Billy could hear a faint rumble. Was there a storm rolling in, or maybe a plane?

Sissy reacted to the rumbling with a loud hiss. Her fins stood on end like the hairs of an angry cat, and a sense of panic set in. Through the clouds, Billy saw four planes, piloted by Hahn Kahn's bandits, quickly approaching them.

In an attempt to stop the planes, Sissy let loose a burst of angry flames from her mouth.

From the ground, Hahn Kahn screamed into his radio, "Don't hurt her, you idiots! Don't hurt her! Use the net—force her to the ground!"

Aboard the USS *Hope*, Captain Curtis, realizing the danger to Billy and Sissy,

loaded the ship's harpoon. A long rope and a huge fishing net were tied to one end of the harpoon.

The Captain waited and watched as Sissy got closer and closer to the ship. He knew that Hahn Kahn wanted to trap her on the ground.

On their last flyby, they were close enough for action. The Captain took aim and fired the harpoon at the lowest-flying plane. The harpoon, dragging the huge net with it, captured all four planes like butterflies in a net.

The harpoon was fastened to the bow of the USS *Hope*, and when the rope tightened, the planes began to spin helplessly in circles.

At just the right time, Captain Curtis cut the rope and sent the planes into an enormous snow bank on the other side of the village.

The Eskimos shouted in victory. Using their dogsleds, they went after a few of the escaping bandits.

From across the ice, the villagers could see Hahn Kahn's truck quickly approaching. The truck was equipped with heavy-duty snow tracks and had a net gun mounted in the rear. Its large, bright headlights resembled a charging beast. The strange sight frightened some of the Eskimos, and they ran away.

Sissy hit the ground hard as she landed on the ice. Billy, tossed from her back, lost his glasses. For a brief moment, he was stunned and searched frantically in the snow for his glasses. He heard the roar of Hahn Kahn's truck as it turned toward Sissy, and two of Kahn's desert bandits took aim with the net gun.

They fired as soon as Sissy was in their sights. The enormous net sailed through the air, stretching open like a giant mouth. Just before the net landed on Sissy, she hurled a fireball at Kahn's truck. It hit the driver's door, ripping it from its hinges.

Hahn Kahn, with his pants on fire, jumped from the truck. It was a funny sight to see as he sat in the snow to put out the flames.

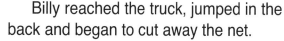

By now Sissy was wrapped tightly in the net and could no longer open her mouth. Hahn Kahn and his bandits quickly loaded her into the back of their truck, his clever plan was working.

Not sure what he was going to do, Billy rushed toward the truck. One thing was certain: he had to free Sissy. He remembered he had the small knife the Captain had given him. As he removed it from his pocket, he remembered the Captain's words. *Sometimes you'll have a need for a knife, especially to cut rope or mend nets. All first mates need a knife.*

Billy reached the truck, jumped in the back and began to cut away the net.

Out of nowhere, Hahn Kahn knocked the knife from Billy's hand. "You made a great effort, kid! But it's all over now. I've won! But I gotta give you credit—Captain Curtis has taught you well."

"Yes, he has. And you won't get away with this," Billy shouted.

Hahn Kahn grinned. "But I *am* getting away with it, and soon I'll have her treasure too! I want to thank you for helping me find Sissy. I couldn't have done it without you and, of course, the Captain." Hahn Kahn laughed as he pushed Billy off the truck, sending him sliding across the ice.

But before Billy slid into the water, Love popped up and stopped him.

As the truck pulled away, Sissy cried for help.

Billy was terrified that Hahn Kahn was actually getting away.

Love said, "Don't worry, Billy. They won't get far!"

Billy could barely hear Love over the deafening sound of a foghorn. The USS *Hope* was plowing through the ice and headed directly toward Hahn Kahn's truck. The ship slammed into the truck, and Kahn's men all tumbled off onto the ice.

Everyone cheered, and Captain Curtis immediately climbed down from the ship. Hahn Kahn shook off the collision and tried to make his escape. That was short-lived, as he bumped into Captain Curtis, who said, "No one touches my first mate or Sissy and gets away with it."

The Captain knocked Hahn Kahn into a snow bank, and the rest of the villagers surrounded his bandits.

Billy rushed over to the Captain and gave him a big hug. Without saying a word, Captain Curtis handed Billy his fishing knife to cut Sissy loose.

As soon as she was free, Sissy took to the air.

Billy, Captain Curtis, and all the villagers smiled as they watched her soaring high into the heavens. With all eyes on Sissy, Hahn Kahn jumped up and pulled Love from the water. He slung her over his shoulder and headed for his truck. "Maybe I lost Sissy, but Love will do for now. She must know where the rest of the treasure lies."

Billy turned around and saw what Hahn Kahn had done. "Stop!" he cried out. Billy dove at Kahn's legs, knocking him down. Kahn lost his grip on Love, and she disappeared through a crack in the ice.

Kahn's eyes blazed with anger. "You meddling little kid!"

Billy knocked Hahn Kahn right in the mouth. He hit the scoundrel so hard that two of his gold teeth flew to the ground.

Wasting no time, One-eyed Jack swooped down and snatched up the teeth. He tucked the booty into the pouch under his wing.

"Billy Pip: one! Hahn Kahn: zero!"

Moments later, Sissy landed alongside Billy and the Captain.

Everyone cheered as they gathered around.

Captain Curtis lit his pipe, looked down at Billy, and asked, "Did you enjoy our trip, Billy?"

"It was magical, sir. I can't believe we are finally here with Sissy."

The Captain put his hand on Billy's shoulder. "Don't forget, it was the journey that made our destination so sweet. It was never really about catching Sissy; it was all about the chase."

"Yes, sir! I'll never forget."

One-Eyed Jack squawked, "Not napping! Squawk! Not napping!"

Sissy purred in agreement.

Everyone smiled.

Dazed and confused, even Hahn Kahn sat up for a split second and smiled goofily.

Billy and the Captain patted Sissy's red mane. She took off, but not before giving everyone another incredible light show.

Little by little, Sissy disappeared into the night sky.

Sounding rather sad, Billy asked, "What now, Captain?"

The Captain puffed on his pipe and said, "Well, I guess it's time to get you home."

Billy's face lit up brighter than the northern lights.

Homeward

West of the lighthouse, the sky was still clear as the sun settled into the horizon. However, a mile or so out on the ocean, a night fog was beginning to form. The seas were calm, and a flock of seagulls followed a boat as it approached the dock.

Inside the cottage, Billy's mother, Maggie, was making dinner. She looked out through her kitchen window and saw the USS *Hope*. She couldn't believe her eyes. She blinked, rubbed them, and blinked again. Sure enough, it was the ship.

Shocked and happy at the same time, she ran out the door. As she reached the dock, she saw Billy, with a crow on his shoulder, waving from the bow of the ship. What in heaven's name was going on?

Puzzled, she glanced toward Billy's skiff, still padlocked in the yard.

The USS *Hope* tooted her foghorn, and Maggie saw a figure waving from the pilothouse. With a look of confusion on her face, she returned the wave.

"Hi, Mom," Billy yelled. "It's great to be home again. Did you miss me?"

Billy tossed the bowline to his mother.

"Billy, what are you doing on that boat?"

Without answering, he climbed down from the ship. He ran over to his mother and gave her a big hug. "Mom, I've been on a great adventure! We battled with Hahn Kahn and his desert bandits! We found treasure! I even beat a giant in a wrestling match! I went to the Arctic and captured Sissy the Sea Serpent!" The words flew from Billy's mouth so fast that he became breathless. "I rode on Sissy's back all through the northern sky."

Maggie shook her head. "Billy, Billy. How's that possible? I thought you were napping in your skiff this afternoon."

One-Eyed Jack squawked, "Napping! Squawk! Napping!"

Maggie did a double take at the talking crow. "My goodness, a talking crow?"

Billy glanced at Faith and looked into the water at Love. They were both giggling.

Maggie's eyes followed Billy's, but what she saw was a lantern and a friendly dolphin—certainly nothing out of the ordinary.

"Well, Mom, I know it's hard to understand. But I'll try to explain everything."

The USS *Hope* tooted her horn. Billy and his mother turned toward the pilothouse and watched Captain Curtis get off the ship.

She gasped. "Oh my goodness!"

With a smile on his face, Captain Curtis approached Maggie and Billy.

Billy said, "Captain Curtis, this is my mom."

The Captain removed his hat and bowed his head slightly. "Good afternoon, Mrs. Pip. It's been a while."

Billy's mother wavered on her feet, and she began to cry.

Confused, Billy asked, "What's wrong, Mom?"

The Captain quickly gave her a big hug and a kiss. She looked at Billy and said, "Son, this captain who took you on your amazing adventure…is your father."

Billy was completely confused, so much so that he almost started to cry. "But… but… you…you *always* told me my father was lost…lost at sea…" While Billy spoke, he slowly pulled off his hat.

Maggie's mouth dropped open. Much to her surprise, Billy's hair was now red… just like the Captain.

She grabbed her son and gave him a big hug.

"Yes, I was lost at sea, son. But my spirit has always been with you."

Maggie nodded. "You were always a good man, Mr. Pip."

Maggie and Billy gave the Captain a long-overdue hug.

After many tears and much laughter, the Captain took out his pipe and lit it.

He hesitated for a moment. "Mrs. Pip, as much I would like to stay, the fog is rolling in and I must go." He stared softly at Maggie and added, "I promise to take Billy on another magical trip. After all, there are many more dragons to hunt, fish to catch, and dreams to chase."

Maggie smiled and said, "I can see that you'll never change, Captain Curtis."

The Captain leaned in and gave her a kiss on the cheek. "And you wouldn't want me any other way, Mrs. Curtis Pip."

She nodded and placed her arm around Billy's shoulder. "And neither would your son."

The Captain turned and said, "See you next time the fog rolls in." He turned and started back to the USS *Hope* with One-Eyed Jack on his shoulder.

Billy broke away from his mother and ran down the dock. Waving good-bye, he stood there watching the USS *Hope* leave.

Billy yelled, "Good-bye, Dad!"

The Captain stuck his head out the pilothouse window. "Remember, First Mate, always carry Hope, Faith, and Love in your heart, and I'll never be that far from you."

One-Eyed Jack squawked, "Hope, Faith, and Love! Squawk! Hope, Faith, and Love!"

In the blink of an eye, the USS *Hope* disappeared into the mysterious Atlantic fog.

Looking out over that wonderful ocean, Billy wondered when and where his next magical trip would take him.

The End

Made in the USA
San Bernardino, CA
06 January 2014